FEELINGS

ISBN 0-89868-344-0–Library Bound
ISBN 0-89868-405-6–Soft Bound
ISBN 0-89868-345-9–Trade

A PREDICTABLE WORD BOOK

FEELINGS

Story by Janie Spaht Gill, Ph.D.
Illustrations by Karen O. L. Morgan

 ARO PUBLISHING

4

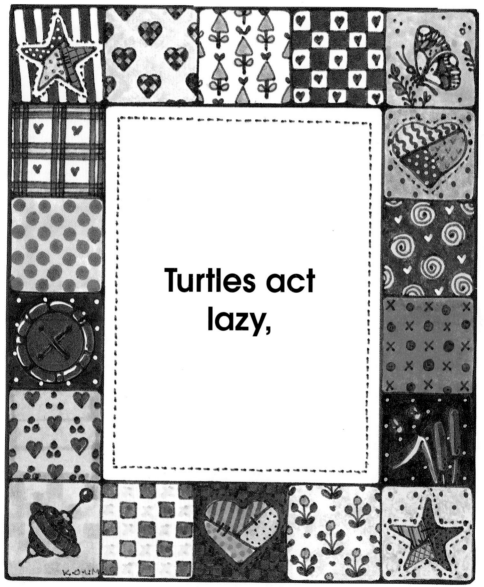

Turtles act
lazy,

5

6

and monkeys
act crazy.

7

8

Bears act
rough,

10

and lions act tough.

11

12

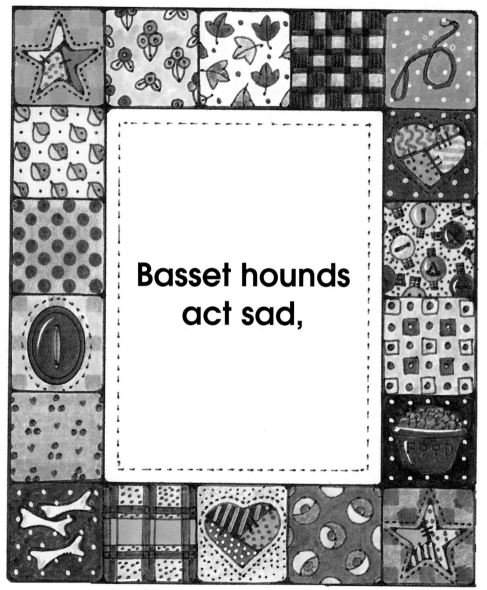

Basset hounds
act sad,

14

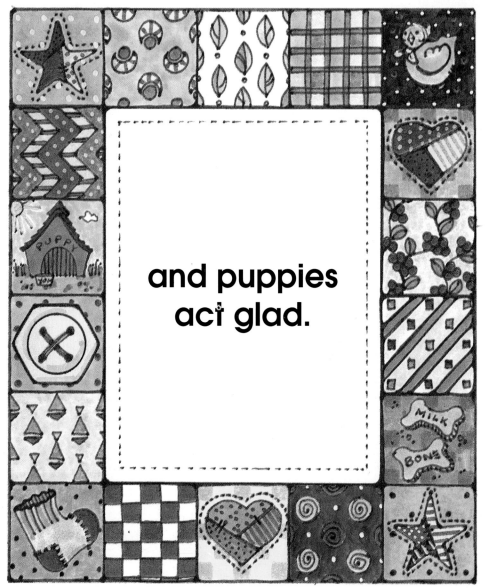

and puppies
act glad.

15

Frogs act jumpy,

18

and bulls act
grumpy.

19

Pigs act greedy,

22

and cats act
sleepy.

Animals have feelings too, just like me and you.